After
the
Moonrise

Rich Lo

muddy boots

Essex, Connecticut

In memory of my sister, Alice Lee, and my parents, Cho Tok Lo and Wai Quen Lo, who kept our family together through tough times in a country and culture they knew little about.

An imprint of Globe Pequot, the Trade Division of
The Rowman & Littlefield Publishing Group, Inc.
4501 Forbes Blvd., Ste. 200
Lanham, MD 20706
www.rowman.com

MuddyBootsBooks.com

Distributed by NATIONAL BOOK NETWORK

British Library Cataloguing in Publication Information available

Library of Congress Cataloging-in-Publication Data available

ISBN 978-1-4930-6434-2 (cloth)
ISBN 978-1-4930-6942-2 (epub)

Printed in Mumbai, India
February 2022

Moonlight pierces the scattered clouds.

A raccoon makes her way toward a distant cornfield.

A skunk climbs out from
a rotting log and joins the
raccoon on her journey.

Startled, bats flutter from under an old bridge.

A coyote howls from
a faraway hill.

The raccoon and skunk come to a wooden gate at the end of an old farm road.

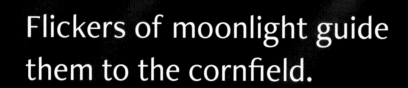

Flickers of moonlight guide
them to the cornfield.

Hidden among the
cornstalks, they
gorge themselves
on sweet kernels.

Suddenly a dog barks.

Lights come on inside
a farmhouse.

The raccoon and skunk
race out of the cornfield.

When the barking stops, the
two head back into the woods,
their bellies full.

They part ways at the skunk's home.

The raccoon turns to look at
the cornfield.

After the moonrise.

Rich Lo

Rich Lo is an award-winning author/illustrator,
and a commercial and fine artist. His work can be
found on packaging and ads for national brands
and on large installations in public buildings.
His first picture book, *Father's Chinese Opera*,
was named an ALA Asian/Pacific American Award
for Literature Honor book. Rich is the author/
illustrator of *After the Snowfall*. That book's
success inspired the creation of *After the Moonrise*.